The Spark Files

Terry Deary trained as an actor before turning to writing full-time. He has many successful fiction and non-fiction children's books to his name, and is rarely out of the best-seller charts.

Barbara Allen trained and worked as a teacher and is now a full-time researcher for the Open University.

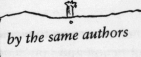
by the same authors

THE SPARK FILES:
1 Space Race
2 Chop and Change
3 Shock Tactics
4 Bat and Bell

The Spark Files

Book Two

CHOP AND CHANGE

illustrated by Philip Reeve

faber and faber

First published in 1998
by Faber and Faber Limited
3 Queen Square London WC1N 3AU

Typeset by Faber and Faber Ltd
Printed in England by Mackays of Chatham plc, Chatham, Kent

© Terry Deary and Barbara Allen, 1998
Illustrations © Philip Reeve, 1998

Cover design: Shireen Nathoo

Terry Deary and Barbara Allen are hereby identified as authors
of this work in accordance with Section 77 of the Copyright,
Designs and Patents Act 1988

A CIP record for this book
is available from the British Library

ISBN 0–571–19369–2

10 9 8 7 6 5 4 3 2 1

For my father, Stan, with love. BA

BE A SAFE SCIENTIST

TIE BACK LONG HAIR, WASH YOUR HANDS AND COVER ANY CUTS AND SCRATCHES WITH PLASTERS BEFORE WORKING WITH FOOD...

ASK AN ADULT TO HELP IF YOU ARE DEALING WITH BOILING WATER OR USING THE COOKER

USE PLASTIC CONTAINERS RATHER THAN GLASS ONES. IF YOU COME ACROSS BROKEN GLASS GET AN ADULT TO HELP YOU CLEAR IT UP... HELP!

NEVER PUT WASHING POWDER OR ANY OTHER CHEMICAL IN YOUR MOUTH

GLURK!

ALWAYS WASH YOUR HANDS AFTER USING CHEMICALS OR HANDLING FOOD

KEEP MOULD IN A SECURELY COVERED CONTAINER, AND THROW THE CONTAINER AWAY UNOPENED WHEN YOU HAVE FINISHED...

GRRRR!

Chop and Change

File 1

Susie Spark
(that's me!)

Beautiful heroine of this tale. They want to build a statue of me but I was afraid of what the pigeons would do to my image

Susie Spark's a lovely girl
Braver than St. George's
dragon
Pretty as a Miss World winner
Brainy too— and I'm not
braggin'.

File 2

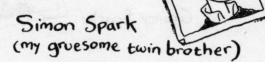

Simon Spark
(my gruesome twin brother)

If he had double the brains
he'd be a half wit. How could someone
as daft as him be my twin?

Cross-eyed, spotty, ugsome thing
For a head he has a pimple
Dad calls him his 'little
                    treasure'
Me, I just call Simon 'Simple'!

File 3

Granny Spark

When she talks about the
Queen we think she means Victoria!
She's so old she can do our history
homework from memory.

Rosy-cheeked and snowy-haired
Granny lives back in the past
Tells us ancient boring stories
'When she used to be a lass'!

File 4

Lolly Lady Lil

Jolly Lollipop Lady. Always laughing but never tells us what the joke is. Favourite trick is stepping out in front of the cars of teachers she doesn't like, keeping them waiting for five minutes... laughing!

When we cross the road to
school
Lolly Lady Lil Steps out
Teachers' cars must wait
forever
Lily laughs... while teachers
Shout!

Chapter 1

You've probably heard about me or read all about it in the papers, when our town of Duckpool was terrorized by the 'Cheerful Chopper', a mad and monstrous axe-person who brought a threat to thousands and sent the bravest boys bolting for their beds. They hid under the blankets and shivered in fear.

Who beat this brute and saved you citizens? Me! Susie Spark. But perhaps some of you haven't heard of me.

WELL, YOU WILL!

It all started one evening when Mother and Father went to a parents' evening at the school. They took my buffoon brother, Sam, and my snooty sister, Sally, with them. They left Granny Spark in charge of me, my twin brother Simon and Baby Spark. Big mistake. If we were attacked by a mad axe-person then Grandmother couldn't be expected to defend us. And that evening we *were* . . . and she *couldn't*!

'Ha! Ha!' Father chuckled as he brushed his hair with the shoe brush and brushed his shoes with the hairbrush. 'You'll be safe enough, Susie!'

'Yes, Father, I'll look after Grandmother and the others.'

'It's not as if Duckpool is a *dangerous* town, with a mad axe-man on the loose!'

'Axe-*person*, Father. The correct term is axe-person.'

But he wasn't listening. 'Did you know my shoes have dandruff?' he asked Mother.

'Did you know your hair has a lovely shine?' she replied. Mother turned to me. 'You have plenty of homework to keep you busy, Susie?'

'Yes, Mother. Science experiments on the subject of "Change",' I told her.

'Simon will help you if you get stuck,' she said.

I could feel my face turning purple at the thought. I would rather kiss a wasp's bum than ask for Simple Simon's help. '*I* will help *Simon* when *he* gets stuck,' I said in my sweetest voice.

Mother patted me on the head (I hate that) and they left. Baby Spark crawled over the floor and pressed the television controller. (Baby Spark enjoys the six o'clock news. A bright Spark, who clearly takes after me.)

Grandmother knitted and muttered, 'When I were a lass we never had no televisions. We used to sit on the

8

floor and look at the wall till it were time to go to bed.'

I turned to Simple Simon. 'Right, brother. Change!'

'I changed when I got home from school,' he said. 'I had to. My trousers were muddy from playing football and . . .'

I stopped him. 'Silence, foolish boy. I meant *Change*. Our science project. Get out that worksheet and I'll show you how to do it.'

Making sugar crystals

1 Tip a glass of water into a saucepan and heat it until it boils.

2 Turn the heat down low.

3 Pour some sugar into the water a little at a time and stir. Keep adding sugar until no more will dissolve. You may need to use 2 or 3 cups of sugar. Tip the mixture into a clean glass.

4 Rub some sugar into a piece of cotton then tie it around a pencil. The length of the cotton should be about the same as the height of the glass. You can weight the bottom of the cotton with a paper clip.

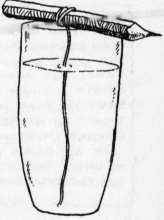

5 Place the pencil across the top of the glass with the cotton hanging into the mixture. Leave it in a warm place.

6 After a few days you will see small crystals on the cotton. These are crystals of sugar.

No sooner had we set up the experiment than Baby Spark cried, 'Goo! Goo!' and pointed a fat finger at the television. The news-reader was looking serious and frightened – seriously frightened – by the newsflash she held in her trembling hand . . .

REPORTS ARE COMING IN OF A MAD AXE-MAN ON THE LOOSE IN THE QUIET SEASIDE TOWN OF DUCKPOOL!

Simon said, 'Gosh!'
Gran said, 'Good grief!'
Baby said, 'Goo!'
I said, 'That should be axe-*person*!'

SORRY – THAT SHOULD BE AXE – *PERSON*. A SHORT FAT FIGURE WITH A LONG HANDLED AXE WAS SEEN RUNNING ACROSS THE PLAYING FIELD OF THE LOCAL SCHOOL. WITNESSES SAID THAT THE DANGEROUS ARMED CRIMINAL WAS LAUGHING WILDLY ENOUGH TO TURN YOUR BLOOD TO MICE... SORRY. I'LL READ THAT AGAIN. THE LAUGHTER TURNED WITNESSES' BLOOD TO *ICE*. POLICE HAVE WARNED EVERYONE TO STAY IN THEIR HOMES, LOCK ALL DOORS AND WINDOWS AND LET NO ONE IN UNTIL THIS CREATURE, NICKNAMED THE CHEERFUL CHOPPER, IS CAUGHT.

I leapt to my feet and ran around the house locking everything. Simple Simon just sat there and laughed. 'Don't panic, Sis! The axe-man wouldn't come after you!'

'I am not panicking – and the words are "sister" and "axe-person", if you don't mind.'

I turned back towards the television . . .

'Oooh! The Queen's coming here!' Grandmother cried. 'I hope she brings Albert with her. Such a handsome man!'

'Hah!' Simon laughed. 'The Queen will think she's seeing double! Old Lil looks just like her!'

SHE WILL PRESENT LOCAL LILLYPOP LODY LAL... ER... I'M SORRY, I'LL READ THAT AGAIN. THE QUEEN WILL PRESENT LOCAL LOLLYPOP LADY LIL WITH THE CBE FOR SERVICES TO DUCKPOOL CHILDREN....

'Huh!' Grandmother grumbled. 'I never got no medals for being a Lollipop Lady for fifty years, man and boy. I was a Lollipop Lady before they was even invented! I had to take my own lollipop!'

'What happened to your lollipop, Gran?' Simon asked.
Grandmother sighed. 'It melted.'

Suddenly there was a rattle at the letterbox. I screamed
– not because I was scared for *myself*, you understand. I
was worried about Grandmother and Baby Spark.

'Aaaagggghhhh!' I cried. 'It's the Cheerful Chopper
come to get us!'

Chapter 2

Simon jumped to his feet and walked into the hallway while I watched him from behind the settee. 'Look at this!' he whispered. 'I've never seen anything like it!'

'What is it?' I gasped as he came back in with a piece of paper in his hand.

'A letter!'

'What?'

'A letter! Whoever heard of a postman calling at this time of the evening?' he said with a shake of his head.

'When I were a lass there were twelve deliveries a day,' Grandmother chuckled.

'Who is it addressed to?' I asked.

'Granny!' he said

Grandmother sliced it open with her knitting needle and read it to us. 'Dear Granny Sparks, I have been watching you and I know where you live. I am in your town and I am coming to get you. It's no good locking your doors. Signed the Mad Axe-man.'

'Simon, you check the doors and I'll lock the cat flap,' I shouted.

When we got back in the sitting room Grandmother was crying. I'd never seen her so upset. 'You'll be all right, Grandmother. We'll look after you,' I said as I put a comforting arm around her shoulders.

'Stop it, I can't take any more. Stop making me laugh. My sides are hurting. You are so easy to fool – not such a bright Spark now, Susie, my girl.' I put a comforting hand round her throat and helped her to her feet.

'What did the letter *really* say?' I asked her.

'I don't know. I didn't have my reading glasses on!' she cackled.

I snatched the letter from the slobbering jaws of Baby Spark. Too late. The mighty maggot had taken a bite from it. I spread it on the table.

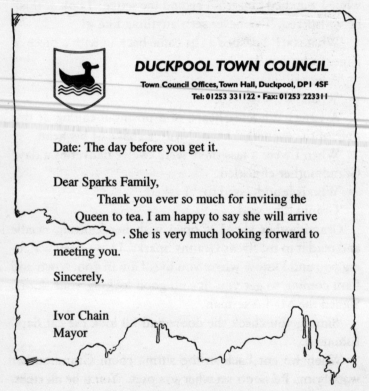

DUCKPOOL TOWN COUNCIL

Town Council Offices, Town Hall, Duckpool, DP1 4SF
Tel: 01253 331122 • Fax: 01253 223311

Date: The day before you get it.

Dear Sparks Family,
Thank you ever so much for inviting the Queen to tea. I am happy to say she will arrive   . She is very much looking forward to meeting you.

Sincerely,

Ivor Chain
Mayor

'The Queen's coming here!' Granny grinned. 'That'll be nice for her. When I were a lass we had kings, of course.'

The baby crawled over to the television and turned on the local news.

WHEN THE QUEEN VISITS DUCKPOOL TOMORROW SHE WILL VISIT SOME LOCAL PEOPLE IN THEIR HOMES. WE HAVE HEARD THAT SHE IS PLANNING TO HAVE TEA WITH DUCKPOOL'S OLDEST RESIDENT.

CLICK

'Gran, who's Duckpool's oldest resident?' Simon asked.

'Probably me,' she replied. 'I'm not quite sure when I was born. But I do know I was very young at the time. Maybe she wants to give me one of those CBE thingies for my work as a Lollipop Lady! I was the CBE of Duckpool – that's Champion Best Ever! If I hadn't attacked that bus with my lollipop I'd have still been doing it today!'

While Grandmother rambled, Simple Simon leapt into action. 'So that letter's true! She's coming here! Clean the kettle and put the house on,' he cried.

'I think you mean the other way round, Simon,' I said.

I didn't see why we should make so much fuss for any visitor. After all, would the Queen make me a cup of tea if I felt like dropping into the palace? I didn't think so. So why should we rush around for her?

'I'm going into the kitchen to do my homework.' I took out my science book and looked at the homework.

I wondered why the teachers always gave me easy

Change
Question 2

Some materials change when they are cooled. What happens to water? Design an experiment to show why frozen pipes burst.
Then explain how you can stop your pipes bursting.

homework to do. Don't they realize how super-brainy I am? Perhaps I need to tell them again. I started to write about the experiment I'd begun when I got home from school.

MY EXPERIMENT

I poured water into a plastic bottle. Then I put a piece of tin foil on the top. I put it in the freezer for a few hours.

When I took it out, the bottle was full of ice. The ice had pushed the tin foil lid off the bottle.

This experiment shows how water expands when it freezes to make ice. If I had put a proper lid on my bottle then it would probably have burst just like a pipe does.

The way to stop your pipes from bursting is to move to a warmer country.

That should do it, I thought, and closed my book. Simon walked in carrying the vacuum cleaner in one hand and Baby in the other.

'Take this, will you,' he said and handed me Baby. I carefully put Baby on the worktop. When you are a scientist you have to be very careful not to have accidents. I didn't want Baby to fall off the worktop so I hooked its dungarees over the mug rack. It was a mistake. Baby could still reach the radio to turn it on. The news-reader sounded even more scared than the one on the television.

THE POLICE HAVE ISSUED ANOTHER WARNING ABOUT THE CHEERFUL CHOPPER IN DUCKPOOL. EVERYONE IS ADVISED TO LOCK THEIR DOORS AND NOT TO ANSWER THEM TO ANYONE. THE CHOPPER IS THOUGHT TO BE A MASTER OF DISGUISE AND WAS LAST SEEN HEADING FOR THE WEST SIDE OF TOWN...

'That's us!' I said. 'Have you checked all the doors, Simon?'

'Yes! They are all locked and we are perfectly safe. A chimp with a chainsaw couldn't get in here.'

In the dark garden owls hooted, a cat howled and an unearthly scent filled the kitchen. 'Susie!' Simon whispered.

'What, Simon?'

'I think Baby's just filled its nappy!'

Chapter 3

The baby grinned at us. 'Poo!' it said.

'Now this is very good timing, Baby Spark!' I said.

'Goo?' it replied.

'We are studying "Change" in school and we are going to "change" your nappy. But first we'll bath you. Simon, take off baby's nappy!'

'Phwoar! No! It stinks!' he moaned.

'The whole house will stink if you don't take it out to the dustbin,' I told him.

'I'm not going out there in the dark with some Cheerful Chopper waiting to turn me into chips!'

I took off the nasty nappy and wrapped it tightly in some newspaper. 'Now, Simon,' I said. 'Show me your homework book.'

Compared to my exercise book, Simon's was as disgusting as Baby's nappy. 'Load of boring questions about soap and changes,' he grumbled.

> **Change**
> Some materials change when they are
> mixed with others. When soap is
> mixed with water then both the soap
> and the water are changed.

'Now, Simon, fill Baby's bath with warm water and test it with your elbow to see if it's right,' I ordered.

'Why my elbow?' he asked.

'Because I say so,' I told him. 'I've watched Father and Mother bath Baby and they always use their elbows.'

I turned to undress Baby while Simon filled the bath. When I turned back Simon was shaking his head. 'I've wet my shirt! It's horrible!'

I sighed. 'You are supposed to roll your sleeve up before you put your elbow in the water, Simon.'

'You never said,' he mumbled.

'What you doing in there?' Grandmother called.

'Bathing Baby!' I told her.

'Want any help?'

'No, Grandmother. You dropped Baby last time, remember?'

'Remember what?'

'Baby being dropped on the floor!'

'What do you want to do a thing like that for? You'll crack the tiles!'

I counted to five to keep my temper and said, calmly, 'Carry on knitting, Grandmother.'

'No, I'm not knitting a Grandmother, I'm knitting a scarf!'

I turned the radio up to drown the sound of me screaming to myself.

WE INTERRUPT THIS PROGRAMME TO INTERRUPT THIS PROGRAMME. LOCAL WOMAN, LAUGHING LOLLIPOP LADY LIL, WAS DUE TO BE PRESENTED WITH THE CBE BY THE QUEEN TOMORROW. BUT THERE WAS CONCERN IN DUCKPOOL TONIGHT WHEN SHE FAILED TO TURN UP AT A PARTY ORGANIZED BY MAYOR IVOR CHAIN. SHE WAS LAST SEEN AFTER SCHOOL, STOPPING BUSES JUST FOR A LAUGH. THERE ARE FEARS THAT SHE MAY HAVE FALLEN VICTIM TO THE CHEERFUL CHOPPER. POLICE ARE MAKING HOUSE-TO-HOUSE ENQUIRIES. UNFORTUNATELY EVERYONE IS REFUSING TO ANSWER THE DOOR BECAUSE THEY THINK THE POLICE ARE THE CHEERFUL CHOPPER IN DISGUISE...

POLICE ARE ASKING THE PUBLIC NOT TO OPEN THEIR DOORS TO ANYONE - EXCEPT THE POLICE WHO ARE NOT THE CHEERFUL CHOPPER IN DISGUISE. AND WE INTERRUPT THIS INTERRUPTION TO EXPLAIN THAT THE CHEERFUL CHOPPER MAY APPEAR DISGUISED AS A LAUGHING POLICEMAN. THE REAL POLICEMEN HAVE PROMISED NOT TO LAUGH - EVEN IF YOU TAKE THEIR BOOTS OFF AND TICKLE THEM. THEY ARE ASKING YOU TO KEEP YOUR RADIO TURNED ON FOR FURTHER NEWS. IF YOU HAVE NOT HEARD THIS ANNOUNCEMENT BECAUSE YOUR RADIO IS TURNED OFF, THEN TURN IT ON NOW.

'Mother and Father are out there on the dangerous streets! Alone!' I said.

'Nah, they're not alone if they're with each other,' Simon said.

'Alone – except for each other,' I said, just a little annoyed.

'And Sally and Sam,' Simon went on.

'Pass me that worksheet,' I said and I put Baby in the bath.

---

1 Throwing and catching wet and dry soap

Throw a bar of dry soap to a friend for him/her to catch. Try this ten times. Count the catches. Now wet the soap and throw it to your friend.

What do you notice?

> *I notice that Baby is hopeless at catching*

Is it as easy to catch when it is wet?

> *Pass*

Why do you think it is dangerous to leave a wet bar of soap on the bathroom floor?

> *You might bump your head on the toilet when you bend down to pick it up*

Wet soap is harder to pick up than dry soap. Wetting the soap has changed it. Never leave a wet bar of soap on the bathroom floor because someone might slip on it

Even you could write better answers than Simon! Look at his second worksheet!

2 Changing soap by putting it in warm and cold water

Get two small pieces of soap that are exactly the same size. Put one in a bowl of cold water and the other in a bowl of hot water. Time how long it takes them to dissolve.

Which one dissolved first?

Don't know. Baby stuffed them in my mouth

Why do you think that happened?

I think I swallowed the bits

Do you think it is better to wash clothes in hot or cold water?

Yes

It is better to wash clothes in warm or hot water because the soap powder dissolves more quickly.

As for his third sheet it is almost too disgusting to show you.

3 Squeezing soap to change it.

Some materials can be changed by heating or cooling them. Others can be changed by squeezing them.
Find a small piece of soap. Look at the shape of it carefully. Now draw it on the sheet.
Squeeze the soap into a different shape. Draw the new shape on the sheet.

← Susie's face

Even though the soap is a different shape can you still use it to wash yourself?

I wouldn't want to wash myself with something as ugly as Susie's face

It doesn't matter what shape the soap is – you can still wash yourself with it.

No thanks.

After all that bathing of Baby and experimenting with soap we had almost forgotten about the Cheerful Chopper. But then, as we poured the soapy water down the sink we heard a sound that made my toes curl with creepiness. There was a soft scratching at the back door.

I put my ear against the cat flap – that was brave of me . . . the Cheerful Chopper's axe could have splintered that wood like a knife cutting through paper. There was no mistaking the sound. A gasping, rasping panting of someone half a metre off the ground, desperate to get in to our house!

Chapter 4

'Listen!' I whispered. I was on my hands and knees. Simon was staring with eyes goggling like gooseberries. Baby crawled across the floor towards me and smiled, showing four teeth – two up, two down.

'Doggie!' Baby gurgled.

'Mad axe-person!' I whispered.

Baby gave a gurgling giggle. 'Doggie!'

I looked up at Simon. 'Where's Boozle the dog?'

'Went out with Mum and Dad. They probably sent him to the paper shop to fetch the evening paper home. That'll be him at the back door! Let him in!' Simon said.

I opened the cat flap and peered out into the darkness. A long wet tongue slithered over my face. It was revolting. If this was the mad axe-person then he smelled just like our dog.

'Where's the paper?' I growled.

'Woof!'

I opened the door and picked up the newspaper from the doorstep. The dog pushed past me wagging his stumpy tail and slobbering all over the floor. He must be the most revolting creature in the world – apart from my brother.

I opened the newspaper. On the front page was the headline:

Lil is Leading Lolly Lady

A photograph of Lil filled half the page. She was laughing and waving her lollipop at a car driver.

As I was walking out of the room Grandmother said, 'The curtains will have to be washed. I can't have the Queen here when me nets aren't gleaming. Go up to my bedroom and fetch me net curtains.'

'Grandmother, the Queen will not be going into your bedroom,' I explained through gritted teeth.

'That's not the point, my girl. *I'll* know they're not clean.'

'I'll do it,' Simon offered and ran upstairs.

I am always suspicious when Simon is being helpful. I'm even more suspicious when he is a long time being helpful. After ten minutes I was super-suspicious.

I raced into the bathroom but it was too late.

'I've put the curtains in the bath to wash them,' he said with a grin. The idiot had put every curtain in the house in the bath.

'How long do you think it will take to do this lot?'

'Dunno. A bit of time.'

'We scientists like to be a bit more accurate than that,' I said very patiently. 'We need a scientific experiment to save us! We need to know which curtains will dry quickest. Then we'll hang those at the front! They're the only ones Her Majesty will see!'

'What experiment, Einstein?'

'Some materials change when they are dipped in water. But not plastic. And that's why we don't make wellies out of wool! We have cotton, wool and polyester curtains here. Your job is to test those three materials!' I quickly wrote down the experiment on a piece of paper.

EXPERIMENT TO TEST WHICH MATERIALS SOAK UP WATER BEST

You need four different types of material: Cotton, Wool, Plastic and Polyester — or any other

Four saucers with two tablespoons of water in each

1. Place a 10cm square of material in each puddle.

2. Take out the material squares and place them on a warm radiator.

Which dries fastest and which slowest?

'Do you think you can do that?' I asked.

'No problem.'

I knew what the results were going to be. I thought the experiment would keep him busy for a while.

IF YOU DON'T KNOW WHAT'S GOING TO HAPPEN IN THE EXPERIMENT THEN TRY IT FOR YOURSELF. BUT DON'T PUT ALL YOUR CURTAINS IN THE BATH.

← WRONG

I left him in the bathroom and went downstairs. As I walked into the living-room there I noticed a corner of the front page I hadn't spotted before . . .

STOP PRESS:

The Duckpool Police are warning of a mad axe-person, the Cheerful Chopper, and have just issued a photo-fit. If anyone recognizes this person will they please notify the police immediately.

I couldn't be sure but I thought I'd seen that photo-fit face somewhere before.

And, underneath the picture I read the chilling words . . .

> The famous Lollipop Lady, Lil, is missing and feared to be a Chopper victim. Mayor Ivor Chain said, 'We've heard reports that a bus caught her outstretched lollipop and sent her spinning into a lamp-post. She may have had a blow to the head, lost her memory and wandered off. We hope so!'
>
> The latest sighting of the madman was in Shave Close.

I looked at my Grandmother and she looked at me. We looked at each other! We both looked at the newspaper. The madman was in our road. He could be looking for our house. He could be looking for *us*.

Chapter 5

Simon ran into the kitchen holding a small square of blue polyester. 'This stuff dries quickest.'

'Polyester!' I said. 'Then the polyester curtains will dry first! As I suspected. Bring them down and we'll stick them in the spin drier.'

Simon brought the curtains down and dumped them on the kitchen table. 'You did well . . . for an idiot! Where did you get the samples of materials?' I asked.

'I cut the cotton square from one of Dad's handkerchiefs,' he said.

'Could be messy when he comes to blow his nose!' I said, cringing at the thought.

'I cut the wool from an old blanket in the dog's bed.'

'And the polyester?'

'Er . . . nothing,' he mumbled.

'The only blue polyester I've seen in this house are my . . .'

Simon turned and began to run out of the kitchen. I ran to the door and screamed after him, 'Knickers!'

Grandmother looked up, startled. 'When I was a lass we never used language like that. We'd have gone to bed with no supper! Of course we never missed it 'cos we never had no supper anyway! Hah!'

I stormed back into the kitchen. I pushed the bundle of curtains into the spin drier. I pressed the switch. The drier groaned and the drier creaked. Then smoke started to drift out of the back and sparks lit up the kitchen. An orange light flashed on the front . . .

I couldn't understand it! One pair of curtains wouldn't overload our machine. I pressed the switch again. This time a message came on in red . . .

I kicked the machine . . .

Ouch!

'See what you've done, Simon?' I called up the stairs. 'We have wet curtains. If the Queen arrives now we'll have nothing up at the windows. We can change materials by wetting them . . . but how do we change them to make them dry with no spin drier?'

'When I were a lass,' Grandmother said, 'we washed everything by hand and we didn't have none of those spin-nie drier thingies. No! We had to blow on the clothes till they was dry. By gum, but we used to have some puff in them days!'

'Grandmother, you are lying,' I said severely.

'Mebbe! Mebbe! But I do remember we had home-made spinning machines when I were a lass. One of the women's magazines had a picture of it!'

'Where's the magazine, Gran?'

'In the attic, of course. When I were a lass we were too poor to have attics. We were too poor to even have a roof!'

'How did you manage?' I asked.

'We slept in a tent in the cellar, of course.'

She was rambling again. I snatched a torch from the sideboard drawer and ran up the stairs. The ladder to the attic was thick with cobwebs and I had to fight my way past some pretty angry spiders, I can tell you.

It was cold and dark up there. Something bat-like fluttered in one corner and something rat-like scuttered in the other corner. I found the pile of old magazines as quickly as I could and shone the torch on the faded covers. The one I wanted was on the top!

I ran downstairs with the magazine and opened it on the kitchen table.

Simon had come out of hiding. 'I've lost Baby!' he said.

'Where did you last see it?' I asked.

'On the kitchen table,' he said. 'Do you think Baby climbed down and slid out of the cat flap?'

I rubbed my eyes wearily. It was one of those nights. I marched into the kitchen, flung open the spin drier door and said, 'Dad's hammers and spanners are in here. He left them under the kitchen table.'

'So who put them in the spin drier?' Simon asked.

I looked under the table where the greasy bag lay. It was empty . . . except for a pink, oil-stained figure. 'Baby Spark! Get out!'

'Goo!' Baby giggled and crawled out.

The spin drier flashed an orange message . . .

I told you I was overloaded! See!

I went back to Grandmother's magazine. There was the advert for the spin drier. I reckoned we could make one of those!

The curtains were too big for a lemonade bottle so I used Father's car-washing bucket and punched holes in it. Simon, Grandmother and I took turns to whiz it round

I was an unhappy housewife until I discovered the **Whizzo** Spin Drier!

So simple to assemble!

1. I just took an empty plastic lemonade bottle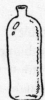

2. Punched it full of holes

3. Cut the top off and tied a boot lace to the end

4. Filled the **Whizzo** with my wet clothes…

5. Whirled it round my head…

6. And ended up with nearly dry clothes! It even gave the dog a free shower!

41

our heads. The curtains were dry enough to iron in no time . . . and the dog got a free bath. The kitchen walls got washed too. I decided to iron the curtains on the kitchen table. They were done in ten minutes.

It would have taken less time but there was a bump in the tablecloth.

Suddenly I said, 'Where's Baby?'

And Simon said, 'I left Baby on the table!'

Well, that sorted the problem of the bump under the tablecloth. It was when I went to the window to hang the curtains that I saw the most terrifying sight that would have turned a brave girl's guts to grape juice.

As I fixed the last curtain hook on the rail I looked out into the darkness. I saw the reflection of my own face and I saw a curious shape in the garden beyond. The Cheerful Chopper's axe was lit by the light from our window. And the words were clear for all to see . . .

Chapter 6

I pulled the curtains tightly together.

'What's wrong?' Simon asked. 'You look as if you've seen a ghost!'

'The Cheerful Chopper is standing outside our window!' I said and my voice seemed to be squeaking like a rusted hinge.

Simon opened the curtains a little and peered through. After a moment he turned and looked at me. 'Nothing there, sis. I guess you imagined it!'

'Telephone the police!' I said and my voice still wouldn't work properly.

'When I were a lass,' Grandmother said, 'we didn't have no telephones. We used carrier pigeons. They were slower, but at least you could eat them when they'd done their job!'

I snatched the phone and pressed it to my ear. It was as silent as the bottom of the Arctic Ocean. 'The line's been cut!'

Simon laughed. 'Bet you never had that problem with pigeons, Gran!'

'What are we going to do?' I asked, trying to get some sense out of the two idiots I was sharing a house with.

'We'd better get tea ready for the Queen, that's what we'd better do,' Grandmother said.

'Tea?'

'Yes, some nice sandwiches. After all, she may arrive tonight. Baby Spark destroyed the bit of the letter that told us what time,' Grandmother said. 'Anyway, it'll take your mind off this Chummy Chipper!'

'Cheerful Chopper.'

'Him as well! Now let's get into that kitchen!'

I looked in the breadbin and pulled out a green loaf. 'Yeuch, it's gone mouldy.'

'I told your father to put it in the freezer. In my day the only way to stop food going mouldy was to eat it.' Grandmother was rambling again.

'I told Dad it wouldn't keep,' said Simon.

'How did you know that?' I asked.

'Because of the results of my experiment,' he said. He was shuffling from one foot to the other. He always does that when he's done something wrong. But what could be wrong with doing an experiment?

'Explain your experiment to me,' I said suspiciously.

'I'll draw it for you.'

'When you leave the jars for a few days they grow mould on them. So you have a mould farm,' he explained.

'Where is this mould farm?' I asked.

'In my bedroom.'

'Go and fetch it, you idiot.'

My stupid brother came back into the kitchen with his four jars of food. You could see the mould growing on some of the food. I knew that bacteria caused the mould to grow.

What's more, I knew that some could be very dangerous. At least Simon had sealed the lids with sticky tape.

'You've seen the mould growing. Now go and throw these jars away in the bin,' I told him.

'But I was reading about how mould helped in the discovery of antibiotics. I had antibiotics when I had a sore throat,' he whined.

He showed me the page from his science book.

In World War I, doctors used antiseptics to clean wounds. These did not kill the bacteria that caused infection. Alexander Fleming (1881–1955) was a doctor who was trying to find a better way to treat wounds. One day in 1928 Fleming discovered a mould that would kill bacteria. This mould is known as penicillin.

'Fleming used to paint with bacteria,' rambled Grandmother.

'What?'

'She's right!' said a surprised Simon.

Bacteria grow in different colours. They can be many colours including red, violet and orange. Fleming used to draw with different bacteria on a special dish. He covered it over and after a few days his picture would grow.

'I expect he couldn't afford paint,' Grandmother said.

We still needed some more bread from the freezer in the garage. Who was going to go and fetch it with the mad axe-person roaming around outside our house? We needed someone very brave . . . or someone very stupid.

'Simon, go and fetch some bread from the freezer. If the mad axe-man is at the front door then it's safe for you to go out of the back door. Go and get the bread while I distract the maniac.'

'Good thinking, sis.' He was out of the back door like lightning.

'Is there anybody there?' I shouted through the front door letter-box.

I could hear a grunting sound and someone gasping for breath. It sounded just like Father when he comes home from jogging.

'Who is it?' I shouted again. I could hear footsteps moving away from the door and round the side of the house. If the mad axe-person caught Simon then it could be serious. We'd never get the bread.

I ran into the kitchen and threw open the back door. 'Run, Simon!' I cried.

Just in time Simon rushed back into the kitchen and I locked the door behind him. 'The Cheerful Chopper almost got me!' he panted.

'It could have been worse. It could have been me out there,' I told him. 'Now give me that bread.'

Chapter 7

You'd think it would be easy to make sandwiches. Not in our house. I left the bread on the kitchen table while Grandmother called us into the living-room to give us instructions.

'The Queen always has her crusts cut off her sandwiches,' she told us.

'That's just cos her false teeth can't cope,' I told her. 'I like crusts.'

'We're not having her going back to Buckingham Palace and telling stories about us!' she gasped.

'What stories?' I demanded.

'She'll be saying, "You'll never believe this, but that Spark family have crusts on their sandwiches. Common as muck!" she'll be saying!'

I turned to my brother for support. 'Well, Simon? What do you think? With crusts or without crusts?'

'Er . . . without crusts, Susie,' he said looking towards the kitchen.

I did think that putting poison in his pop was too kind for a traitor like him. 'Why?' I asked.

'Because Baby Spark and Boozle the dog have been fighting over the bread. They've sort of pulled the crusts off! You haven't got much choice, Susie!' he said.

'Wha-a-a-a-a-t!' I wailed. But he was right. The two animals – a four-legged smelly one and a two-legged one in a nappy – sat on the kitchen floor and looked guilty.

I rescued what was left of the bread and put it on the table. 'Butter!' I said to Simon.

'Goo!' Baby Spark said, holding up two greasy hands.

'Shlurp!' Boozle dog said, licking two greasy lips. The butter dish was empty.

'The greedy turnips have eaten it!' I cried. 'You'll have to get some more, Simon!'

'I'm not going to the corner shop for butter if there's an axe-person loose!' Simon said. 'He might get me next time!'

'When I were a lass we used to make all our own butter,' Grandmother said. 'Butter didn't come in packets in them days.'

We had a choice. Give the Queen dry bread and get gossiped about in Buckingham Palace, or make some butter. 'How do you make butter, Grandmother?' I asked.

'Well, you start off with a cow,' she said.

'We haven't got one,' I said. 'And I think the corner shop was fresh out of them. We've plenty of milk. What do I do next?'

'It's all in your great-grandmother's cookery book. It's there on the bookshelf behind the television,' she said.

I found the old, brown bound book and blew off the

thick layer of dust. I looked up 'butter' in the index and opened it at the well-thumbed page.

Make your own butter

You could start off with a cow, but its easier to start with cream from the shop.

Pour some cream in a clean jar
and put the lid on.
Shake the jar and watch the
cream change into butter.
Pour off the liquid.
Add a pinch of salt if you wish.
Don't worry if you don't get
results immediately.
Keep shaking.
At least it'll keep you fit!

I left Grandmother to butter the bread while I turned on the television to see a round-faced, frowning man with a fringe of hair round the side of his head and another fringe under his nose.

MY LIL WAS A LOVELY WOMAN. SHE WAS QUEEN OF THE MAY BACK IN 1956. ALWAYS LAUGHING. ALWAYS LAUGHING AND HAVING FUN. JUMPING OUT IN FRONT OF THOSE BUSES WAS HER FAVOURITE, OF COURSE.

SNIFFLE!

'I remember the Queen of the May!' Grandmother shouted from the kitchen. 'We used to dance around the Maypole on Duckpool village green! Then we picked the prettiest girl to be May Queen!'

'Yes, Gran, but can I listen to the news!' I snapped. 'They have a picture of the Cheerful Chopper suspect. Look!'

Grandmother stood in the doorway and watched as terrifying pictures flashed on the screen . . .

When Baby Spark saw the fourth picture it screamed in terror, 'Goo!' and pointed at the television screen.

'Aaaagh!' Simon cried. 'What a nightmare.'

Grandmother said, 'I think that one looks rather pleasant!'

EEK!

Chapter 8

I snapped the television off. Those faces were enough to give you nightmares. Suddenly Simon said, 'It's interesting, this "Change" stuff! Everything changes when you think about it. Add water to the Queen's tea bag and you *change* the water. You change its colour and you change its taste.'

'That reminds me. We should be laying the table and getting the tea things ready. If she doesn't come tonight then Mother and Father can have the tea when they get back from parents' evening.'

'They're not getting our sandwiches!' Simon cried. 'Not after all the trouble we've gone to.'

'They'll be dry and hard by tomorrow,' I argued.

'Yeah!' he said, snapping his fingers. 'We need something to *stop* change!'

'Let's look up "stopping change" on the computer,' I told Simon.

Simon ran upstairs to fetch the portable computer from my bedroom. We needed to find out how to keep the food fresh because we didn't know when the Queen was going to arrive.

'We can't bottle or can the sandwiches. I suppose we could freeze them,' I suggested.

'Mmmm! Frozen sandwiches. Very tasty,' said Simon.

'How do we keep our sandwiches fresh when we go on a picnic?'

FOOD CAN BE KEPT FRESH IN MANY WAYS. IN THE MIDDLE AGES PEOPLE USED TO KEEP MEAT FRESH BY COVERING IT IN SALT. THEY ALSO USED TO BUILD ICE HOUSES TO KEEP FOOD FRESH IN THE SUMMER. FRUIT CAN BE KEPT FRESH BY BOTTLING OR CANNING.

'We put them in a sandwich box.'

'We'll try different things and see which works best.'

We wrapped one lot of sandwiches in tin foil, one in cling film, and put some more in a sealed sandwich box. 'I think we should leave some out in the open air just to see what happens,' said Simon.

It was the most intelligent thing he'd said all day.

'At least we don't have to worry about keeping the milk fresh. We can put that in the fridge,' I said.

'When I was young there was only one way to keep milk fresh,' said Grandmother.

'What was that?' I asked.

'Keep it in the cow,' she cackled.

I needed to find a way to keep Grandmother busy while I sorted out how to get a message to the police about the mad axe-person in the garden.

'You could put the sandwiches in brandy to keep them fresh,' she said. 'They might taste even better then!'

'Where does she get these ideas from?' I asked.

'It's on the computer,' said Simon.

IN 1805 ADMIRAL LORD HORATIO NELSON WAS KILLED AT THE BATTLE OF TRAFALGAR. AS A HERO OF THE NATION, THE SAILORS WANTED TO BRING HIM BACK TO LONDON FOR BURIAL. IT WAS A LONG JOURNEY AND THEY HAD TO STOP HIS BODY FROM ROTTING. THEY SEALED IT IN A BARREL OF BRANDY. WHEN THEY REACHED LONDON THEY FOUND THE BODY WAS BEAUTIFULLY PRESERVED. NELSON WAS BURIED AND THE SAILORS DRANK THE BRANDY.

'I feel sick.'

'I feel hungry,' Simon said. I glared at my brother.

'Grandmother, can you make some more sandwiches for the human dustbin please?' I thought that would keep her in the kitchen out of trouble. Simon and I walked into the dining-room and started to lay the table.

We could hear Grandmother clattering about in the

kitchen. I could never work out why she made so much noise. We could hear cupboard doors slamming and crockery smashing. The dog yelped when she stood on him. And then I heard the back door slamming. I froze.

'Simon, why do you think Grandmother opened the back door?'

'To let someone in?' he said.

'But who?'

'It's only the Queen come for her tea!' Grandmother called from the kitchen.

Chapter 9

A large woman in a yellow and white plastic coat stood in the doorway. She held a pole in her hand and looked around the room with blue staring eyes. 'You're not the Queen!' I squawked.

She turned her great blue eyes on me. 'She *was* back in 1956!' Grandmother said from the kitchen. 'She was May Queen!'

'Lollipop Lil!' I gasped. 'You're Lollipop Lil!'

'Never heard of her,' the woman said and waved her axe dangerously. The axe head was on a red and yellow striped pole.

'The old lady said I was the Queen. And she should know! Are you arguing, fat face?' she asked me.

'No!' I said quickly.

'Your Majesty! No . . . your Majesty.'

'No . . . your Majesty!'

'We've got your tea all ready for you . . . your Majesty,'

Grandmother said with a chuckle. 'Sit down and have a cuppa and a sandwich.'

Lil threw her axe on to the table and turned two cups, three saucers and a plate into dust. 'Don't mind if I do!' she said. She sat at the table and grabbed a handful of sandwiches. 'Here! This bread's got no crust on!'

'You don't have crusts on your sandwiches in Buckingham Palace,' I told her.

'Don't I?'

'You seem to have lost your memory,' I said. 'Maybe your lollipop was smashed by a passing bus, you got bumped on the head and lost your memory! You *think* you're the Queen – and the rest of Duckpool thinks you're a mad axe-person on the loose!'

'Do they? Why do they think that?' she asked, wide-eyed and wondering.

'Because your lollipop was smashed into the shape of an axe head!' I said and pointed to the wooden pole with its smashed sign that lay on the table.

The wild blue eyes narrowed. 'That's my sword of state!' she said. 'I'm the Queen and that's my sword of state! It's for bashing enemies of the state. Look! Only a sword could do this sort of damage!'

She raised it into the air and smashed it down on the table. Two more cups would never hold tea again. 'Go and get help!' I said to Simon.

'I'm not going out there! There's a mad axe-person loose!'

'No, there *isn't*! Lollipop Lil's the mad axe-person and she's in here! She'll smash the house if you don't get help!'

'You'll have to keep her entertained,' Simon said.

'How?'

'Look . . . here's my science book. Find some experiment to amuse her.'

It sounded crazy but it was my only hope. I opened the book and it fell open at . . .

Have fun with soap bubbles

1 Make a mixture of 1 spoonful of water to 3 spoonsful of washing up liquid.
2 Bend a piece of wire into a loop.
3 Dip the wire in the mixture and blow your bubbles.
4 Try making the wire into different shapes and see what happens.

Lil was fascinated by the bubbles. She began laughing in her mad way. Then she picked up her lollipop and began to prod the bubbles. 'Pop! Hee! Hee!' she cackled.

The lollipop went through the bubble and she didn't notice that she had swept Mum's best china cat off the mantelpiece.

I snatched a pen from my school bag and tore a sheet from Simon's exercise book.

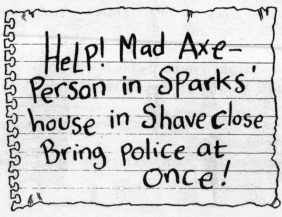

Help! Mad Axe-Person in Sparks' house in Shave Close Bring police at once!

I stuffed the note into Simon's hand. 'Run to the corner shop. Get them to phone from there!'

Simon nodded. He headed for the door. Suddenly the lollipop axe swung round and caught him round the neck. 'What you got there, boy?' Lollipop Lil asked.

Simon handed the note over.

Lil looked at it. 'You can't take this note. Your Queen won't allow it!'

'No, your Majesty.'

'It's too dangerous,' she said. Suddenly her voice dropped to a whisper. 'There's a mad axe-person out there!'

Chapter 10

I groaned. How could I explain to her that *she* was the mad axe-person? I couldn't. Instead I turned back to Simon's book 'True Spy Stories'. There was one chapter in there that had caught my eye. It offered us one small chance of getting a message out to our rescuers.

Secret Messages

Spies often need to get messages to each other.
They sometimes write in code or they use invisible ink.
You don't need to go to a shop to buy invisible ink.
You can make it at home.

You need: the juice of a lemon, a thin paintbrush,
a piece of paper.
Dip your paintbrush in the lemon juice and write your
message. Put more lemon juice on the paintbrush
after every letter. Leave the message to dry.
When you want to read your message put it face down
in the oven. (The oven should be heated to 175°C or
Gas Mark 4.) It should take about ten minutes.
This works because the heat
of the oven burns the lemon
juice but not the paper. Burning
changes the lemon juice and
makes it go brown.

← BEFORE

AFTER → HELP!

Did you know . . . Prisoners of war used to
use sweat and saliva as invisible ink.

EURGH!

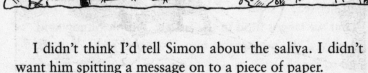

I didn't think I'd tell Simon about the saliva. I didn't
want him spitting a message on to a piece of paper.

It didn't take me long to write the message on a piece of

paper. I wrote a shopping list in between the secret message.

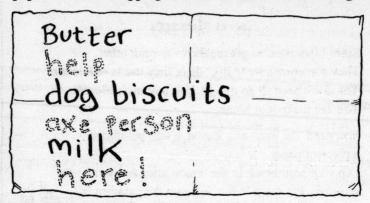

Butter
help
dog biscuits
axe person
milk
here!

I strolled into the sitting-room and winked at Simon. He winked back. The boy can be very stupid sometimes.

Lil and Grandmother were staring at the blank television screen. 'Do you want me to turn it on?' I asked.

'We don't need television. In our day we had to make our own entertainment,' said Lil.

'I used to love decorating. Once you'd finished painting the walls you could watch it dry. Hours of fun that was.' Grandmother was definitely cracking up.

'And we used to make rugs from rags,' Lil said. 'If the cat caught enough mice then we could make a fur rug. Those were the days,' Lil added.

'We may have been poor but we were happy,' Grandmother sighed.

I didn't think I could take much more of this. 'Simon, you need to go to the shop for some food. The Queen will want her tea!' I said.

'But we've got food in the fridge,' Simple Simon said.

I waved the message at him. 'Not *this* food. You *need* to go to the shop!'

Lil spotted the piece of paper. 'What have you got there?'

'A shopping list . . . your Majesty.'

'Show it to me!'

I handed her the paper and held my breath.

'That looks OK,' she said and gave me the paper.

I grabbed Simon by the ear and dragged him out of the chair. 'You have to go to the shop,' I said very slowly and winked.

'Have you got something in your eye, Susie?'

If the boy had a brain, he would be dangerous. I pushed him into the kitchen and explained about the secret message.

'Cor, that's really clever. Why didn't I think of that?' he asked.

'Because you were not blessed with a great brain like me.' I gave him the message and shoved him out of the front door. The letter-box opened almost immediately and I could see Simple Simon's eyes.

'Hey, sis.'

'What?'

'Exciting, innit?'

Chapter 11

'Where's the little boy gone?' Lollipop Lil asked and her eyes were rolling like pink, ten-pin bowling balls.

'To the shop,' I told her. All the time my mighty brain was working on a way to keep her quiet till the police arrived.

'Can I get you anything else to eat?' I asked.

'Yes!' she said brightly. 'Call one of the palace servants. Tell them I'll have an egg for my supper!'

'When I were a lass,' Grandmother said, 'the only eggs

we got were ones we pinched from nests in the hedgerows. And a blue tit's egg doesn't fill a very big hole, I can tell you!'

'When I were a lass,' Lollipop Lil replied, 'the only eggs we got were frogspawn eggs! They served them up for school dinners and called it sago pudding!'

'Well, when I were a lass,' Grandmother said angrily, 'the only eggs we got was spiders' eggs! And we ate them raw on a bed of fresh spiders' webs!'

'Well, when I were a lass . . .' the Cheerful Chopper began.

'Stop!' I cried. 'I think there's a hen's egg in the kitchen!'

The two women looked at me. 'No need to shout, Susie. I'm not deaf and neither is the Queen, are you, your Majesty?'

'Eh?' the Lollipop Lady said.

I went into the kitchen. Where had I seen that egg? Under the kitchen sink. It looked a little odd but I stuck it in an egg cup and served it on a plate.

'Goo!' Baby Spark said.

'Yes,' I sighed, 'it does look a little gooey, but she'll never notice.' I took it through to the living-room and put it on the table in front of Lollipop Lil.

That smashed china on the table would upset Mother and Father when they got home. I went back into the kitchen to get a dustpan and brush from under the sink. That's when I found a piece of paper under the saucer that had held the egg. It was one of Simon's worksheets. I read it with a feeling of horror . . .

Change. Experiment to show that washing powder can eat an egg.

You will need: two jam jars, an egg, biological and ordinary washing powder

1 Boil an egg for ten minutes, let it cool and peel it.
2 Put a tablespoon of biological powder into one jar, and a tablespoon of non-biological powder into the other. Label the jars.
3 Put about eight tablespoons of warm water into each jar.
4 Cut two pieces of egg white (the same size) and put one in each jar.

5 Put the lid on and leave them in a warm place for about two days. When you look at the pieces of egg white you should see that the one in the biological washing powder is smaller than the other piece. This is because the enzymes in the powder break the particles in the egg into smaller particles. These small particles then dissolve in the water. The enzymes in your stomach work in the same way.

NB Do not eat the egg, it may make you ill.

I ran back into the living-room. Lollipop Lil sat at the table. There was a startled expression on her face and dribbles of white foam coming from her mouth.

'You poisoned her, Susie lass,' Grandmother smirked. 'Good idea. That'll teach her to come in here smashing our second-best china.'

'That egg, Lil! Don't eat any more!'

The Cheerful Chopper looked at me. 'Who's Lil?'

'I mean . . . your Majesty! Don't eat the egg!'

'It's delicious! The chef seems to have invented a new sauce!'

'It's . . . it's . . . it's an enemy of the state!' I said wildly. 'Trying to poison you! Wash your mouth out with fresh water! Quickly!'

The woman used her pole to heave herself to her feet. She brushed past Grandmother and stumbled towards the kitchen. It was just her bad luck that Baby Spark was crawling through the door to see what was going on. Lollipop Lil tripped over Baby Spark and flew head-first into the kitchen.

'Ooooh!' she cried.

'Goo!' Baby Spark giggled.

There was a great crash as the Lollipop Lady landed against the kitchen table. Then there was a dreadful silence.

'She's dead,' I whispered.

'I just hope she hasn't damaged that table,' Grandmother mumbled.

Then there was a soft groaning from the kitchen. 'Oh! Deary me! Where am I?'

I looked at the woman sitting up and rubbing her head. 'Are you all right, your Majesty?' I asked.

'Majesty? Me?' she asked. Then she burst into peals of laughter. 'Bless you, luvvie, I'm Lollipop Lil! I haven't been a Majesty since I was May Queen in 1956!' She scrambled to her feet.

'Goo!' Baby Spark cried as Lil flashed her frilly pink knickers.

'Sorry about this, love! The last thing I remember I was controlling the traffic and a bus hit me lollipop! Eeeeh! It's dark out there. Must be late. Time I got home to get my Stanley his tea.'

She bustled past me and through the living-room. She flung open the front door. A man stood there in a scarlet robe with a gold chain around his neck. Lil barged past him and into the night.

'Good evening,' the man said to me. 'I'm your mayor, Ivor Chain. I have here this year's May Queen, Tracey Tubb,' he explained, waving at a girl in a dress that would look good on a Christmas tree fairy. 'You'll have got my letter telling you she is coming for tea tonight?'

'May Queen?' I said. 'I thought it was the Queen queen!'

'Can we come in?' he asked.

'No,' I said and slammed the door hard enough to rattle his chain.

73

Chapter 12

I ran back to the kitchen for the dustpan to sweep the mess from the table. 'A bit of glue would soon put that lot right,' Grandmother chuntered.

'Oh, yes! Yes! Yes!' I prayed. 'A bit of glue on your lips would soon put you right too!' I was not in a good mood. When I heard a knocking on the door it was more than I could bear. I picked up the brush. Mayor or no mayor he was going to see how it fitted up his nose.

I flung open the door. 'Hi, sis!' Simon grinned. 'I got the secret message through to the police!'

I dragged him into the house by the front of his blazer. 'I have solved the problem of the Cheerful Chopper all by myself, thank you. I didn't need the police, or you or anyone!'

'Goo!' Baby Spark giggled.

'Oh . . . all right. Baby helped a little bit. Now get out of my way while I sweep up this mess!'

Simon shrugged. 'I'll go into the kitchen to finish my science homework.'

'You'll have to do it without my help. Can you manage that, Simple Simon?'

'Oooh! You shouldn't call your brother "simple",' Grandmother said. 'Say you're sorry!'

I took a deep breath. 'Simon . . . am deeply, truly sorry that you are simple. Now get into the kitchen!'

He wandered off and left me to tidy the room. The Cheerful Chopper's pole lay on the floor and I propped it beside the kitchen door. It was plain to see it was just a school crossing lollipop with the 'St . . .' of 'Stop' snapped off. I don't know why everyone was in such a panic.

I took the broken china into the kitchen to drop it into the bin and looked at Simon's experiment. 'I've learned so much about "Change" tonight I reckon I'll get a top mark for this,' he said cheerfully.

I squinted at his notes.

My experiment about ice-bergs

For this experiment you need an
iceberg (or ice cube)

1. I put my ice cube in a cup and
filled it up with water

2. I left the cup in the kitchen to
see what would happen when it
melted.

3. I thought the water would
overflow but it didn't. I saw
that the ice cube FLOATED
but most of it was
UNDERWATER

Baby Spark pulled itself up to the table and spilled ice-
cubes on to the tiles of the floor. 'You can clear that up,
Simon,' I said.

Before he could move, the back door rattled. Simon jumped up and pulled the bolts. Dad strode into the kitchen. He was smiling happily. 'Good reports at the school,' he said. 'It seems you're quite a bunch of bright Spa-a-a-a-a-a-ghhhhh!'

He stepped on to an ice-cube and shot towards the living-room door. His feet rose to the ceiling and he plummeted towards the floor. Mother said, 'Training for an Olympic diving medal are we?'

But Father's eyes were glassy as a plate of tripe. He rose slowly to his feet and grabbed for the door frame to hold himself up. He missed. His flailing hand caught the broken crossing-patrol lollipop and he used it to hold himself upright. Suddenly he giggled. 'Hee! Hee! Hee!'

There was a hammering at the front door. 'Go away!' Grandmother cried. 'We've got a man trying to hang on to an axe here!'

'Don't worry, madam!' a voice called through the letter-box. 'We got your invisible ink message. We'll get him.'

Crassssh!

Splllllinter!

The front door burst off its hinges and four large policemen crammed into the room. They surrounded Father and handcuffed him firmly. One snatched the lollipop pole and said, 'I arrest you on suspicion of being the Cheerful Chopper!'

'Hee! Hee! Hee!' Father giggled. 'I could be! I don't really know who I am!'

He was dragged out into the night while Sam and Sally pushed the door back in place. Mother stared at the door. 'Someone will have to tell the police about their mistake,' she said.

I looked at Simon, he looked at Sally, she looked at Sam and Sam looked at Grandmother. 'But not tonight, eh?' Grandmother said.

'Not tonight,' we agreed.

So that's the *true* story of the Cheerful Chopper and my part in his capture. I want you to know that because it didn't appear like that in the newspapers the next day. I was furious when Boozle dropped the morning paper on the back doorstep and I read it.

But *you* know the truth now. Don't you?

Simon is simple and I am the real heroine. That's how it always was and how it always will be.

Some things *never* change.

DUCKPOOL DAILY

Brave Boy Is Stopper Of Chopper!

Bright youngster Simon Spark of Shave Close in Duckpool is a hero this morning. Last night he single-handedly saved his Gran, his sister, his dog and a baby from the mad axe-person known as the Cheerful Chopper. When the Chopper burst into his house he wrote a message in secret ink and delivered it to the nearest adults. Then he went back into the kidnap house to comfort his terrified family.

Last night police arrested a man who is being held for questioning. The man stated, 'I can't remember my name, but I'm pretty sure I'm the Queen.' Buckingham Palace have denied that this is true.

Simon's teacher, Miss Fitt, said, 'Simon's a brave boy and a bright boy. He used our science experiments on Change to create that invisible ink. I'll make sure he gets top marks for his science this term. We're all very proud of him.'

**Here is a list of the science experiments in this book.
Did you try them all for yourself?**

Making Sugar Crystals, p.9
Freezing Water, p.19
Wet and Dry Soap, p.26
Warm and Cold Soap, p.27
Changing the Shape of Soap, p.28
Which Materials Soak up Water Best?, p.32
Make Your Own Spin Drier, p.41
Making a Mould Farm, p.45
Make Your Own Butter, p.51
Have Fun with Soap Bubbles, p.62
Invisible Ink for Secret Messages, p.65
How to Make Washing Powder Eat an Egg, p.69
Icebergs, p.76

**If you have enjoyed this Sparks family adventure,
why not try the others in the series?**

Book One: Space Race, 0 571 19368 4
Book Three: Shock Tactics, 0 571 19370 6
Book Four: Bat and Bell, 0 571 19371 4

These books are available from all good booksellers.
For further information please contact:

The Children's Marketing Department
Faber and Faber
3 Queen Square
London WC1N 3AU

Science Notes

Science Notes

Science Notes

Science Notes

Science Notes

Science Notes

....

....

....

....

....

....

....

....

....

....

....

....